Favorite Fairy Tales

TOLD IN FRANCE

Favorite Fairy Tales

TOLD IN FRANCE

*Retold from Charles Perrault
and other French storytellers
by*
VIRGINIA HAVILAND

Illustrated by
ROGER DUVOISIN

Boston   LITTLE, BROWN AND COMPANY   *Toronto*

These stories have been translated and retold from the following French sources:

THE TWELVE DANCING PRINCESSES, from CONTES DU ROI CAMBRINUS by Charles Deulin (Paris, E. Dentu, Editeur, Libraire de la Société des Gens de Lettres, 1874).

PUSS IN BOOTS and THE SLEEPING BEAUTY IN THE WOOD, from HISTOIRES OU CONTES DU TEMPS PASSÉ by Charles Perrault (1697).

DRAKESTAIL, from AFFENSCHWANZ ET CETERA. VARIANTES ORALES DE CONTES POPULAIRES FRANÇAIS ET ÉTRANGERS compiled by Charles Marelle (2nd ed. Westermann, 1888).

BEAUTY AND THE BEAST by Mme. Le Prince de Beaumont in CONTES DE FÉES TIRÉS DE C. PERRAULT, DE MMES. D'AULNOY ET LE PRINCE DE BEAUMONT (Paris, Libraire Hachette & Cie, 1875).

LIBRARY OF CONGRESS CATALOG CARD NO. 59-7346

Ninth Printing

Published simultaneously in Canada
by Little, Brown & Company (Canada) Limited

PRINTED IN THE UNITED STATES OF AMERICA

Contents

*for all the children and their librarians
whose demands are responsible for this book*

The Twelve Dancing Princesses

ONCE UPON A TIME there lived in a small French village a young cowherd named Michel, who had no father or mother. As he was handsome, with blue eyes and black hair, the village girls all admired him. When he drove his cows to pasture, they often called to him. But Michel would only go on without looking at them. The truth is that he thought them very homely. He had heard about beautiful Princesses, and dreamed of marrying one of them.

One day, just at noon when the sun was hottest, Michel ate his piece of dry bread for dinner and went to sleep under an oak tree. He dreamed that a beautiful lady, dressed in gold, came to him and said, "Go to the castle of Beloeil and you shall marry a Princess!"

That evening Michel told his dream to the farm people. They only made fun of him.

The next day at the same hour, Michel went to sleep again under the same tree. The lady appeared to him a second time, and said, "Go to the castle of Beloeil and you shall marry a Princess!"

Again Michel told of his dream, and his friends laughed in his face. Never mind, he thought; if the lady should appear a third time, I will obey her.

The following day, about two o'clock in the afternoon, the little cowherd came down the road, singing as he drove his cows back early to the stable.

In a great rage, the farmer began to scold Michel, who only replied, "I am leaving."

Michel made his clothes into a bundle, said good-by, and set forth bravely. Through the valley, toward the castle of Beloeil, he trudged on. He wondered what lay ahead for him?

There was, indeed, something important.

It was known that in the castle of Beloeil lived twelve beautiful Princesses. And they were as proud as they were beautiful, and so truly royal that they could feel a pea in their beds, even through ten mattresses.

It was known, too, that they lived like Princesses, and never rose until noon. Twelve beds they had, all in the same room. But what was most strange was that, though every night they were locked in by three bolts, every morning their satin shoes were worn out.

When asked what they did at night, the Princesses always answered that they slept. No one ever heard any noise, and no one could understand how the shoes wore themselves out!

At last the Duke of Beloeil had his trumpeter announce that whoever could discover how his

daughters wore out their shoes should choose one of the Princesses for his wife.

On hearing this, a crowd of Princes came to try their luck. They watched all night behind the open door of the Princesses' room, but next morning the young men were gone, and no one could say what had become of them.

When Michel arrived at the castle, he went straight to the gardener and asked for work. The man had just dismissed his garden boy, so, although Michel did not look like a very strong boy, the gardener hired him. He thought the boy's good looks would please the Princesses.

Michel's first duty, when the Princesses arose, was to give each one a bouquet. He placed himself behind their door, with twelve bouquets in a basket. The Princesses took them without even looking at him—except Lina, the youngest, who admired him with her dark, velvety eyes.

Michel knew that all the Princes had disappeared while trying to learn the secret of the

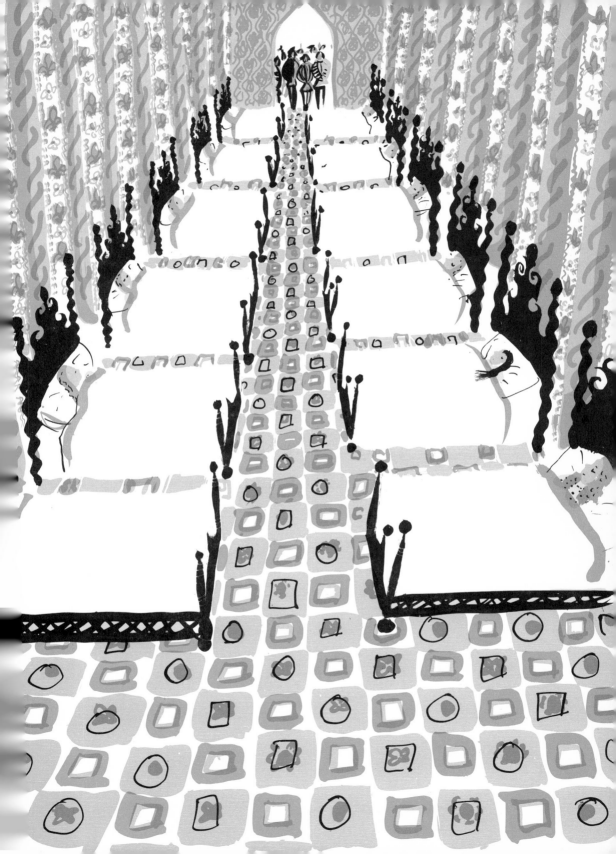

shoes. But Princess Lina's beautiful eyes gave him a great desire to try, himself.

Michel now had a new dream. The lady in gold came to him again, holding in one hand two young trees, a cherry laurel and a rose laurel. In her other hand she held a little golden rake, a little golden pail, and a silken towel.

She said to him, "Plant these little trees in two large pots, rake them with the rake, water them with the pail, and dry them with the towel. When they have grown as tall as a girl of fifteen, say to each of them, 'My beautiful laurel, with the golden rake I have raked you, with the golden pail I have watered you, with the silken towel I have dried you.' . . . Ask then for whatever you wish, and the laurels will give it to you."

Michel thanked the lady. When he awoke from his dream he found the two laurels beside him. Carefully he obeyed the lady's orders.

The trees grew fast. When they were as tall as a girl of fifteen, Michel said to the cherry laurel, "My lovely cherry laurel, with the golden rake

I have raked you, with the golden pail I have watered you, with the silken towel I have dried you. . . . Show me how to become invisible."

That evening, when the Princesses went to bed, Michel followed them, barefoot, and hid under one of the twelve beds.

The Princesses set to work opening cupboards and boxes. They put on the most beautiful dresses, and turned all around to admire themselves in their mirrors. From his hiding place, Michel could see nothing, but he could hear the Princesses skipping about and laughing.

At last the eldest said, "Be quick, girls; our dancing partners will be waiting."

When Michel dared peep out, he saw the twelve sisters splendidly dressed, with satin shoes on their feet, and in their hands the bouquets he had brought them.

"Are you ready?" asked the eldest.

"Yes," replied the other eleven, and took their places in line behind her.

The eldest Princess clapped her hands three times and a trap door opened. They all disappeared down a hidden staircase, and Michel hastened to follow. As he was walking close to Princess Lina, he carelessly stepped on her dress.

"There is someone behind me," cried the Princess, "holding on to my dress!"

"Stupid!" said her eldest sister. "You are always afraid of something. Some nail has caught your dress."

Down, down, down they went. At last they came through a passage to a door closed by only a latch. The eldest Princess opened it. They went out into a beautiful wood, where the leaves were spangled with drops of silver. Beyond that was another wood, where the leaves were sprinkled with gold. From there they went through a third, where the leaves were strewn with diamonds.

Michel saw next a large lake. On its shore awaited twelve little rowboats, decorated with flags. In each one sat a Prince, grasping the oars.

Each Princess entered a boat, and Michel slipped in with Princess Lina.

The boats moved along rapidly. But Lina's, being heavier, lagged behind.

"We don't go so quickly as usual," said the Princess. "What can be the reason?"

"I don't know," answered the Prince. "I'm rowing as hard as I can."

Ahead lay a fine castle, splendidly lighted. From it sounded lively music. In a moment the boats landed. The Princes gave their arms to the Princesses, and they all entered the castle.

Michel followed them into the ballroom. The sight dazzled him—the mirrors, the lights, the flowers, and the rich hangings. Hiding in a corner, he admired the grace and beauty of the Princesses as they danced. He thought Lina, with her velvety eyes, the most beautiful and lovable. And how eagerly she danced! It was plain that she loved dancing better than anything else.

Poor Michel envied those handsome young men with whom Lina danced so gracefully. But he did not know how little reason he had to be jealous.

These young men were really the Princes who had tried to learn the Princesses' secret. The Princesses had given each of them a drink, to enchant them into forgetting everything but the love of dancing.

Everyone danced on till the shoes of the Princesses were full of holes. After a supper of the Princesses' favorite dishes, they went back to their boats.

Again they crossed the wood with the diamond-strewn leaves, the wood with the gold-sprinkled leaves, and the wood whose leaves were spangled with drops of silver. For proof of what he had seen, Michel broke off a small silver branch. Lina turned around at the noise it made.

"What was that noise?" she asked.

"It was nothing," replied her eldest sister. "It was only the screech of the owl at the castle."

Back at the castle, Michel slipped ahead and ran up the staircase, reaching the Princesses' room ahead of them. He opened the window and slid down a vine into the garden. Just as the sky was becoming light, he set to work.

That day, when Michel made up the bouquets, he hid the branch spangled with silver drops in the flowers for the little Princess. When Lina discovered it, she was much surprised. However, she said nothing about it.

In the evening, the twelve sisters went again to the ball. Michel followed and crossed the lake in Lina's boat. This time the Prince complained that the boat seemed heavy.

"It is the heat," replied the Princess. "I, too, have been feeling very warm."

During the ball, she looked everywhere for the garden boy, but in vain.

As they came back, Michel gathered a branch from the wood with the gold-sprinkled leaves. Now it was the eldest Princess who heard the noise it made in breaking.

"It's nothing," said Lina—"only the cry of the owl."

The next morning, Lina found the gold-sprinkled branch in her bouquet. This time she asked
the garden boy, "Where does this come from?"

"Your Royal Highness knows well enough,"
answered Michel.

"So you have followed us?"

"Yes, Princess."

"How did you manage it? We never saw you."

"I hid," replied Michel.

The Princess was silent a moment. Then she
said, "You know our secret—be sure to keep it!"
She threw down a bag of goldpieces. "Here is
something to keep you quiet." But Michel only
walked away without picking it up.

For three nights, Lina neither saw nor heard
anything unusual. On the fourth, however, she
heard a noise in the wood with diamond-strewn
leaves. The next noon there was a branch from
it in her bouquet.

She took Michel aside and said to him, crossly,
"You know what my father has promised to pay
for our secret?"

"Yes, I know, Princess."

"Don't you mean to sell it to him?"

"No."

"Are you afraid?"

"No, Princess."

"What makes you keep quiet about it?"

Michel was silent.

Lina's sisters had seen her talking to the garden boy and made fun of her.

"What keeps you from marrying him?" asked the eldest. "You would become a gardener, too. It is a pretty profession. You could live in the cottage at the end of the park, and help your husband draw water from the well. When we get up in the morning, you could bring us our bouquets."

Then Princess Lina became very angry. When Michel gave her a bouquet, she accepted it coldly. Michel was most respectful and never raised his eyes to her. Yet nearly all day she felt him at her side without ever seeing him.

One afternoon Lina decided to tell everything to her eldest sister.

"What!" said that one. "This rogue knows our secret and you waited this long to tell me! I shall get rid of him at once."

"But how?"

"Why, by having him taken to the tower with the dungeons."

Lina and the eldest sister decided to discuss this with the other ten sisters. All agreed with the eldest that Michel should go to the tower.

Then Lina declared that if they touched a hair of the garden boy she would go and tell their father the secret of the holes in their shoes!

So instead it was arranged that Michel should go to the ball. At the end of supper he would take the drink, which would enchant him like the others.

Now Michel had been present, invisible, when the Princesses talked about this. He had made up his mind to take the drink. He would sacrifice himself thus for the happiness of the one he loved.

But, in order to look well at the ball, he now

went to the laurels and said: "My lovely rose laurel, with the golden rake I have raked you, with the golden pail I have watered you, with the silken towel I have dried you. . . . Dress me like a Prince."

A beautiful pink flower appeared. Michel picked it. In a moment he found himself clothed in velvet as black as the eyes of the little Princess. The blossom of the rose laurel adorned his jacket.

Thus dressed, he went that evening to the Duke of Beloeil. The duke gave him leave to try to discover his daughters' secret. Michel looked so fine that no one recognized him as the garden boy.

The twelve Princesses went upstairs to bed. Michel followed. He hid behind the open door, waiting for the signal to leave. This time he did not cross in Lina's boat. He gave his arm to the eldest sister.

During the evening, Michel danced with each in turn. He moved so gracefully that everyone was delighted with him. At last, the time came for him to dance with the little Princess. She

found him the best partner in the world, but he dared not speak a single word to her.

When the satin slippers were worn through, the fiddles stopped. The dancers all sat down at the banquet table. Michel was placed next to the eldest sister and opposite Lina.

The sisters gave Michel the most delicious food and drink, and the most flattering compliments.

At last, the eldest sister made a sign. One of the pages brought in a large golden cup.

Michel threw a last look at the little Princess. He accepted the cup and lifted it to his lips.

"Don't drink!" Lina suddenly cried. "I would *rather* be a gardener's wife!"

Michel at once flung the contents of the cup behind him. He sprang over the table and fell at Lina's feet.

The other Princes then fell likewise at the knees of the Princesses. Each chose a husband and raised him to her side. The charm was broken!

The twelve couples entered the boats, which had to cross back many times in order to carry

over the other Princes. They all went through the three enchanted groves. When they had passed through the underground door, they heard a great noise, as if the fairy castle were tumbling down.

They went straight to the Duke of Beloeil, who had just awakened. Michel held forth the golden cup and revealed the secret of the holes in the shoes.

"Choose, then," said the duke, "whichever Princess you prefer."

"My choice is already made," replied Michel. He held out his hand to the youngest Princess.

But the Princess Lina did not become a gardener's wife. Instead, Michel became a Prince!

Puss in Boots

ONCE A MILLER left to his three sons a mill,
a donkey, and a cat.

The eldest took the mill and the second the
donkey. The youngest had only the cat. The poor
young fellow was quite unhappy at his poor lot.

"My brothers," said he, "may do well by join-
ing together. But after I have eaten my cat and
made a muff of his skin, I must die of hunger."

The cat, who heard all this, said to him: "Do
not be sad, my good master. You need only give

me a bag and have a pair of boots made for me
so that I may scamper through the brambles. You
shall see that you have not done so badly as you
imagine."

The cat's master had often seen him play clever
tricks to catch rats and mice. He would hang by
his feet, or hide himself in the meal, and play
dead. So the lad did not lose all hope of being
helped.

When the cat received the boots, he pulled them
on with a grand air. Then he put the bag about
his neck, held its strings in his two forepaws, and
went out to hunt for rabbits. He put bran and
lettuce into his bag and stretched out beside it
as if he were dead. He waited for young rabbits,
who had not yet learned the tricks of the world,
to crawl into the bag and eat what he had put
there.

Scarcely had he lain down when he gained what
he wanted. A foolish young rabbit entered the
bag. Puss, drawing close the strings, killed him
without pity.

Proud of his catch, Puss carried it to the King's palace, and asked to speak with His Majesty.

He was shown into the King's rooms. Making a low bow, the cat said:

"I have brought you, sir, a rabbit, which my noble lord, the Marquis of Carabas"—that was the title Puss was pleased to give his master—"has commanded me to present to Your Majesty from him."

"Tell your master," said the King, "that I thank him, and that his present gives me a great deal of pleasure."

Another time the cat hid himself in a field of corn, holding his bag open. When a pair of partridges ran into it, he drew the strings and thus caught both of the birds. He gave them to the King as he had given him the rabbit. The king received the partridges happily, and ordered some money to be given to Puss.

The cat continued for two or three months to carry game to His Majesty. One day, when Puss

knew that the King was to drive along the river with his daughter—who was the most beautiful Princess in the world—he said to his master, "If you will now follow my advice, your fortune is made. You have nothing to do but wash yourself in the river—I shall show you where—and leave the rest to me."

The Marquis of Carabas did what the cat advised, without knowing why. While he was bathing, the King passed by. The cat began to cry out as loudly as he could:

"Help! Help! My Lord Marquis of Carabas is drowning!"

At this, the King put his head out of the coach window. He saw that it was the cat who had so often brought him such good game. He told his guards to run at once to the aid of the Marquis of Carabas.

While they were dragging the young man out of the river, the cat came up to the King's coach. He told the King that as his master was washing in the river, some robbers had run off with his clothes. The Marquis had cried, "Thieves! Thieves!" several times but no one had heard him. (Actually, the clever cat himself had hidden the clothes under a great stone.)

The King commanded his men to run and fetch one of his best suits for the Marquis of Carabas.

The fine clothes suited the Marquis, for he was well built and very handsome. The King's daughter took a secret liking for the Marquis. When he cast two or three respectful and tender glances upon her, she fell deeply in love with him.

The King invited the Marquis of Carabas to come into the coach and take the air with them. The cat, overjoyed to see his plan beginning to succeed, marched on ahead. Meeting some farm workers who were mowing a meadow, he said to them, "Good people, you who are mowing, if you do not tell the King that the meadow you are mowing belongs to My Lord Marquis of Carabas, you shall be chopped as fine as mincemeat."

The King did not fail to ask the mowers to whom the meadow belonged.

"To My Lord Marquis of Carabas," they answered. The cat's threat had made them terribly afraid.

"You have a fine place," said the King to the Marquis of Carabas.

"Yes," replied the Marquis, "this is a meadow which always gives a good harvest."

The cat, still running on ahead, now met some reapers. He said to them, "Good people, you who are reaping, if you do not tell the King that all this corn belongs to the Marquis of Carabas, you shall be chopped as fine as mincemeat."

The King, who passed by a moment after, wished to know to whom all that corn belonged.

"To My Lord Marquis of Carabas," replied the reapers.

The King was still more impressed.

The cat, going on ahead, said the same words to all he met. The King grew astonished at the vast lands held by the Marquis of Carabas.

Puss came at last to a stately castle. The master of this was an ogre, the richest ever known. He owned all the lands which the King had been riding through.

The cat had taken care to find out who this ogre was and what he could do. He asked to speak with him, saying smoothly that he could not pass so near his castle without paying his respects.

The ogre received him as politely as an ogre could, and made him sit down.

"I have been told," said the cat, "that you have the gift of being able to change yourself into any sort of creature. You can, for example, turn yourself into a lion or an elephant."

"That is true," answered the ogre roughly. "To prove it, I shall now become a lion."

Puss was so terrified at the sight of a lion so near him that he at once leaped out on the roof. And not without trouble and danger, because of his boots. These were of no use for walking upon the smooth tiles.

A little while later, when Puss saw that the ogre was no longer a lion, he came down and admitted he had been very much afraid.

"I have been told, also," said the cat, "but I cannot believe it, that you have the power to take on the shape of the smallest animal. I have heard, for example, that you can change yourself into a rat or even a mouse. I must say, I think this impossible."

"*Impossible!*" cried the ogre. "You shall see."

The ogre then changed himself into a mouse and began to run about the floor. Puss instantly fell on the mouse and ate him up.

Meanwhile the King, as he passed the ogre's fine castle, desired to go into it. Puss heard the noise of His Majesty's coach running over the drawbridge.

He ran out and said to the King, "Your Majesty is welcome to this castle of My Lord Marquis of Carabas."

"What, My Lord Marquis!" cried the King. "And does this castle, also, belong to you? There can be nothing finer than this court and all that surrounds it. Let us go in, if you please."

The Marquis gave his hand to the Princess and

followed the King, who went first. They passed into a great hall, where they found a magnificent feast. This the ogre had prepared for his friends. They were that very day to visit him, but now dared not enter, knowing the King was there.

His Majesty was as charmed with the Lord Marquis of Carabas as his daughter, who was so much in love with him.

The King said to the Marquis, "It is only for you to say, My Lord Marquis, whether you will be my son-in-law."

The Marquis, making several low bows, accepted the honor which His Majesty offered. That very day he married the Princess.

Puss became a great lord, and he never ran after mice any more—except for fun.

Beauty and the Beast

THERE WAS ONCE a rich merchant who had three daughters. The girls were all beautiful, but the youngest was so very beautiful that when she was little everyone called her Beauty. The name stayed with her when she grew up.

The two older sisters were jealous of Beauty. The youngest daughter was more lovely to look at than her sisters. She was also more kind and generous. The others spent their days in idle play and made fun of their younger sister, who loved music and books.

Suddenly the merchant lost all his great fortune. He had left only a poor country cottage, a good way from the town. He told his children that they would have to move there and work in order to live.

At the cottage, Beauty rose at four o'clock every morning. She cleaned the house and prepared the food. When she had finished these duties, she read, played her music, or sang while she spun. Her two sisters, on the other hand, were bored to death. They rose at ten o'clock, went out walking, and spent their time feeling sorry for the loss of their fine clothes and their friends.

For a year the family lived quietly. Then one day the merchant heard that one of his trading ships, which he had believed lost, had at last come into port.

The two older girls begged their father to go to the ship at once and to buy for them dresses, fur-pieces, and every sort of trinket. Beauty was quiet. She knew that all the money the ship's goods could bring would not satisfy her sisters.

"You are not asking for anything," Beauty's father said to her.

"You are good to think of me," she replied. "I will ask you to bring me a rose, since there are none growing here."

On arriving at the port, the merchant found he had been cheated. He had to return to the country just as poor as when he left.

The merchant was about thirty miles from home when it began to snow. The wind grew so strong it twice threw him off his horse. As night fell he knew he was lost in a great wood. He feared he would die of hunger or cold, or be eaten by the wolves which howled around him.

Then through a long line of trees a bright light glimmered. He hurried toward it and discovered that it shone from a great palace.

He was surprised to find no one in the palace courtyards. His hungry horse saw an open stable and rushed to a feast of hay and oats, while the merchant went on into the palace. Still he met

no one. In a large hall he found a fire and a table covered with food, but set for only one person.

For a long time the merchant waited for someone to come. Finally, at eleven o'clock, hunger overcame him and he ate a chicken in quick mouthfuls. Becoming bolder, he left the hall and went on through several richly furnished rooms. At the end of these, he found one with a good bed. As it was after midnight and he was very weary, he closed the door and lay down.

It was ten o'clock in the morning when he got up. He was astonished first to find beside his bed a new suit of clothes to replace those which the storm had ruined. "Surely," he said to himself, "this palace belongs to some good fairy, who has taken pity on me in my ill luck."

Looking through the window, he saw arbors of flowers where before there had been only snow.

He returned to the great hall where he had dined and saw a little table set for breakfast. "Thank you, good fairy," he said aloud, "for thinking of my breakfast."

After drinking his chocolate, the good man went out to look after his horse. As he passed under a rose arbor, he remembered that Beauty had asked him for a rose, so he broke off a branch which bore several blossoms. As he did so, he heard a great noise. Coming toward him was a beast, so horrible that it made him shake with fear.

"You are an ungrateful man!" cried the beast in a terrible voice. "I have saved your life by receiving you into my palace. For my pains, you steal my roses, which I love better than anything in the world. In return you shall die, within a quarter of an hour!"

The merchant fell to his knees and begged, "My Lord, pardon me! I did not intend to offend you by picking a rose. One of my daughters especially asked for it."

"I am not called 'Lord,' but 'the Beast,' " answered the monster. "I am willing to pardon you if one of your daughters will die in your place. If not, you must promise to return here in three months."

The good man had no intention of giving up one of his daughters to this monster. He thought: At least, I shall have the pleasure of seeing them once more. So he promised to return.

The Beast then said he could leave as soon as he wished. "But I don't want you to go empty-handed. Go back to the room where you slept. There you will find a big chest. You may put in it whatever pleases you and I will have it carried to your home."

The merchant returned to the room. Finding many goldpieces, he filled the big chest. He closed it and then rode away on his horse, as sad now as he had been happy when he found this place—although he was rich again.

The horse picked his way through the forest, and in a few hours carried the merchant to his little house. His daughters crowded around him, but instead of enjoying their kisses, the merchant began to weep. He held the branch of roses out to Beauty. "Take these roses, Beauty," he said.

"They have cost your poor father dearly."

When he told his family what had happened, the two older sisters screamed at Beauty: "See what you have done! And you do not even cry!"

"That would do no good," replied Beauty. "Why should I weep for the death of my father? He will not die. Since the monster is willing to accept one of his daughters, I will give myself to him. I shall be happy saving my father."

"But," said Beauty's father, "I shall not allow you to die. I am old and can live only a little longer. I shall return."

"No, Father!" cried Beauty. "You cannot prevent my going to the palace with you. I would rather be eaten by this monster than die of grief at losing you."

When Beauty and her father were ready to leave, the two sisters rubbed their eyes with an onion to make themselves cry. Only Beauty did not weep.

The horse carried them through the forest, and by evening brought them to the palace lights.

Beauty and her father went together into the great hall. This time they found a table set for two.

Beauty's father had no appetite, but Beauty, forcing herself to seem calm, sat down at the table and served. The Beast had provided well for her. She thought, "He wishes to fatten me before eating me."

When they had finished dining, they heard a great noise. Beauty could not help shivering when she saw the horrible beast. But she tried to be brave. When the Beast asked if she had come willingly, she told him, trembling, that she had.

"You are good, and I am much obliged to you," said the Beast. "You, merchant, will leave tomorrow morning, and must never return. Good night, Beauty."

"Good night, Beast," she replied.

"Ah, my dear," said the merchant, kissing Beauty, "I am half dead with fright. You must let me stay here in your place."

"No, Father," said Beauty, firmly. "You must

return in the morning and leave me to Heaven's help."

That night, Beauty dreamed that a lady said to her: "I am pleased with your bravery, Beauty. Giving your life to save your father's life will not go unrewarded."

The next morning, after her father had gone, Beauty decided to walk through the beautiful palace.

On one door she found written the words BEAUTY'S ROOM. She opened it hastily, and was dazzled by what she found. What pleased her most was a large case filled with books and a harpsichord with many sheets of music.

"No one wants me to be unhappy," she said aloud. Then she thought, cheerfully: If I had only one day left to live here, no one would have provided all this.

This thought helped her. She opened the bookcase and saw a book on which was written in gold letters:

Make your wish; speak your command—
You are queen of all here.

"Alas," she said, sighing, "I wish only to see my poor father and to know what he is doing now."

To her surprise, a great mirror suddenly appeared before her. In it she saw her home, which her father was entering, with a very sad face! Her sisters were meeting him.

In a moment the picture was gone. But Beauty began to think that the Beast was very kind. Perhaps she had nothing to fear.

At noon, she found the table set. While she ate, she heard soft music, though she saw no one.

At evening, as she was about to sit down at the table again, she heard the Beast coming. Again she trembled.

"Beauty," said the monster, "are you willing to have me see you dine?"

"You are the master," replied Beauty, shaking.

"No," said the Beast. "You are the one in command here. You have only to tell me to go away, if I displease you. I'll go at once. Tell me, do you not find me very ugly?"

"You are so good," said Beauty, "that when I think of you, you don't seem to me to be ugly."

Beauty ate well this night. She had almost lost her fear of the monster—until he asked, "Beauty, are you willing to be my wife?"

She was slow to answer, being afraid of making him angry, but finally she said, "No, Beast."

The poor monster gave a sigh so heavy that it sounded through the entire palace. But Beauty was calm, for the Beast said to her sadly, "Good night, then, Beauty."

"Alas!" she thought. "It is a pity he is so ugly; he is so good!"

Beauty spent three peaceful months in the palace. Every evening the Beast visited her and every day Beauty discovered some new goodness in him. She became used to his ugliness, and even found herself looking forward to nine o'clock in the evening, when the Beast never failed to come.

One thing, only, bothered Beauty. This was that the monster always asked her, before leaving, if she would be his wife. He seemed very sad when she said no. One night she told him, "You make me sad, Beast. I should like to be able to marry you, but I am too honest to let you think it would ever happen. I'll always be your friend. Try to be content with this."

"I must," answered the Beast, "for I know that I am horrible. But I love you so much. Yet I am happy that you are willing to stay here. Promise that you will never leave me."

Beauty was sorry to hear these words, for she had seen in her magic mirror that her father was ill with grief at losing her, and she wished to see him again.

"I should like to promise you this," she said to the Beast, "but I long so much to see my father."

"Then I will send you to your father," answered the monster. "You shall stay with him, and your Beast shall die of sorrow."

"No," said Beauty. "I love you too much to

wish to cause your death. I promise to return in eight days."

"You shall be home tomorrow morning," said the Beast. "But remember your promise. You will have only to place your ring on a table at bedtime to bring you back here in the morning. Farewell, Beauty."

The Beast sighed his heavy sigh and Beauty went to bed, sorry for having saddened him.

When Beauty awoke in the morning, she found herself in her father's house. The merchant heard her and was overjoyed at seeing his dear daughter. Soon Beauty learned that her sisters had married while she was away. They were just now arriving with their husbands.

The girls were full of envy when they saw Beauty dressed like a Princess. Their jealousy grew when they learned how happy she was. Off they went into the garden. There they asked themselves, "Why is this little creature more fortunate than we? Are we not more handsome?"

"Sister," said the elder. "I have an idea. Let's try to keep Beauty here longer than her eight days. The stupid Beast will be so angry that he'll devour her."

"Good, sister!" replied the other. "But to keep her, we shall have to pretend that we love her."

When the eight days were gone, the two sisters seemed so unhappy at Beauty's leaving that she promised to stay another eight days.

During the tenth night at her home, Beauty dreamed that she was in the palace garden. The Beast was lying there on the grass, almost dead. She woke up with a start and began to weep.

"Am I not wicked to sadden the Beast who has shown me such kindness? Is it his fault that he is so ugly? He is good, and that is more important. Why do I not wish to marry him? Well, I'll not make him unhappy any longer."

With these words, Beauty put her ring on the table and went back to sleep. When she woke up in the morning, she saw with joy that she was in the palace of the Beast. She dressed in her best

clothes, to please him, and waited for nine o'clock.

The clock struck nine, but the Beast did not appear. Beauty was afraid. She ran through the palace, crying aloud. Looking everywhere, she then remembered her dream and ran into the garden. There was the poor Beast, stretched out with his eyes shut. Forgetting his ugliness, she bent down to him.

The Beast opened his eyes and said to Beauty, "You forgot your promise. The sorrow of losing you made me decide to starve to death. But I die happily, since I see you again."

"No, dear Beast, you shall not die," said Beauty. "You shall live to become my husband."

Scarcely had Beauty said these words than she saw the palace light up brilliantly. Fireworks and music began to sound gaily through the garden. When Beauty turned to look again at the Beast, what a surprise!

The ugly Beast had disappeared. In his place stood a handsome Prince, who thanked her for breaking his enchantment.

Beauty asked him where the Beast was. "You see him before you," replied the Prince. "A wicked fairy doomed me to keep the form of a Beast until a beautiful girl should agree to marry me. You are the only one in the world to find that I am good. I offer you my heart."

Beauty gave her hand to the Prince and he led her into the palace. There, to her joy, she found in the great hall her father and her sisters, brought by the fairy who had appeared in her dream.

"Beauty," said this great fairy, "come take your reward for your good choice. You are to become a Queen.

"As for you, ladies," said the fairy to Beauty's sisters, "I know your wickedness. You are to become statues at the gates of the palace. I give you no other punishment than seeing Beauty's happiness. You will stand there until you recognize your faults."

The Prince then married Beauty. She lived with him long and in perfect happiness.

The Sleeping Beauty
in the Wood

ONCE UPON A TIME a King and a Queen were very unhappy because they had no children. As the years passed they grew sadder and sadder.

But at last, after many years, the Queen had a daughter. Everyone rejoiced, and a very fine christening was held for this Princess. She had, for her godmothers, all the fairies to be found in the whole kingdom—which were seven. They were invited in order that each should make her a gift, according to the custom for fairy godmothers. The King and Queen knew that in this way the Princess would grow up with the best qualities anyone could imagine.

After the christening, all the company returned to the King's palace, where a great feast was ready for the fairies. On the table before each of them was a magnificent setting of heavy gold—a spoon, a knife, and a fork, all made of pure gold with a pattern of diamonds and rubies.

As they were sitting down at the table, there came into the hall a very old fairy, who had not been invited. No one had seen her for more than fifty years, so she was believed to be either dead or under a spell.

The King ordered a place set for the old fairy, too, but he could not give her a spoon, knife, and fork of gold, because pieces had been made for only seven fairies. The old fairy fancied she had been insulted, and growled threats between her teeth.

One of the young fairies, who sat by her, heard how the old fairy grumbled. She feared the old fairy might give the little Princess a bad gift— so, when they rose from the table, she hid behind the hangings. The young fairy wanted to be last to speak, in order to undo, as much as she could, any evil which the old fairy intended.

Now all the fairies began to make their gifts to the Princess. The youngest, for hers, said that the Princess should be the most beautiful person in the world. The next said that she should have the wit of an angel. The third, that she should have charm in everything she did. The fourth, that she should dance gracefully. The fifth, that she should sing like a nightingale. And the sixth, that she should play all kinds of music perfectly.

The old fairy's turn came next. With her head shaking—more with anger than from old age— she said that the Princess would prick her hand with a spindle and die of the wound. This terrible gift made the whole company shudder. They all began to cry.

At this instant, the young fairy came out of her hiding place and said, "Be assured, O King and Queen, that your daughter shall not die. It is true that I cannot undo all of what my elder has just done. The Princess shall indeed prick her hand with a spindle. But instead of dying, she shall fall into a deep sleep, which shall last a hundred years. After a hundred years, a King's son shall come and wake her."

The King, to avoid this bad luck, at once forbade, on pain of death, anyone to spin or even to have a spindle in the house.

Fifteen years later, when the King and Queen were away at one of their country houses, it happened one day that the young Princess was running up and down the palace. She climbed from room to room and came finally to the top of the tower. Here there sat spinning a good old woman who had never heard of the King's command against spindles.

"What are you doing there, goody?" asked the Princess.

"I am spinning, my pretty child," said the old woman, who did not know her.

"Oh!" said the Princess. "This is very pretty!

How do you do it? Give it to me, so I may see if I can do it, too."

But no sooner had she taken the spindle than it stuck into her hand, and she fell down in a swoon.

The good old woman cried out for help. People came from all sides and threw water on the Princess's face. They loosened her clothes, struck her on the palms of her hands, and rubbed her temples. But nothing would bring her to herself.

Now the King, who had returned, heard the noise and climbed to the tower. He recalled what the fairies had said. Knowing that it must be, he had the Princess carried into the finest room in his palace and laid upon a bed all embroidered with gold and silver.

One would have taken the Princess for a little angel, she was so very beautiful. Her fainting had not taken away the color from her face. Her cheeks and her lips were red. Her eyes were shut, but she was breathing softly. This proved she was not dead. The King commanded the court to let her sleep quietly till her hour of awakening should come.

At this time the good fairy, who had saved the life of the Princess by putting her to sleep for a hundred years, was far away in another kingdom. She learned what had happened from a little dwarf who had boots in which he could go seven leagues in one stride. The fairy left at once for the palace of the Princess. In an hour she was seen arriving, in a fiery chariot drawn by dragons.

The King handed her out of the chariot. She looked about and approved everything he had done. But, as she was very wise, she thought that the Princess, when it was time for her to awaken, would be greatly alarmed at finding herself alone in the palace. So she touched with her wand everything in the place—the governesses, maids of honor, gentlemen, officers, cooks, errand boys, guards, pages, and footmen. She also touched all the horses in the stables, with their grooms. She touched the great dogs in the stableyard and little Pouffe, the Princess's spaniel, which lay close to her on the bed.

As soon as she had touched them, they all fell

asleep. They would not awaken before the Princess needed them. The very spits at the fire, as full as they could be of partridges and pheasants, fell asleep; and the fire, also.

All this was done in a moment, for fairies are not long at their work.

Soon there had grown up all around the park such a vast number of trees, great and small, brambles and thorn bushes, twining one within another, that neither man nor beast could pass through. Nothing could be seen but the very tops of the towers, and those only from a great distance.

At the end of a hundred years, the son of the King then ruling, who was of another family, was out hunting. He was curious about the towers he saw above a great thick wood.

The Prince asked many people about this. Each one answered differently. Some said it was a ruined old castle, haunted by ghosts. Others said that witches had their night meetings there. The

most common opinion was that an ogre lived there, who imprisoned all the little children he could catch.

The Prince was at a loss, not knowing what to believe, when a very old man spoke to him: "Many years ago I heard from my father (who had heard my grandfather say it) that there was in this castle a Princess. She was the most beautiful ever seen. She had been put under a spell, and was to sleep there a hundred years—until a King's son should waken her."

The young Prince felt all afire at these words. He went off at once to see if they were true. Scarcely had he advanced toward the thick wood when all the great trees, brambles, and thorn bushes gave way to let him pass. He walked up a long avenue to the castle. To his surprise, none of his people could follow. The trees closed behind him again as soon as he had passed through, but he went boldly on his way. A young Prince in love is always brave.

He came into a great outer court. What he saw

there might have frozen the most fearless person with horror. There was a frightful silence. Nothing was to be seen but stretched-out bodies of men and animals, all seeming to be dead. He knew, however, by the red faces of the guards, that they were only asleep. Their goblets, in which some drops of wine remained, showed plainly that they had fallen asleep while drinking.

The Prince then crossed a court paved with marble, went up the stairs, and came into the guard chamber. Guards were standing in rows with their guns upon their shoulders, snoring loudly. He went on through several rooms full of gentlemen and ladies, all asleep, some standing, others sitting.

At last the Prince came into a chamber all glittering with gold. Here he saw upon a bed the finest sight he had ever beheld—a Princess, who appeared to be about fifteen years of age, and whose bright beauty had something of Heaven in it. He approached with trembling and admiration, and fell down before her upon his knees.

And now, as the enchantment was at an end, the Princess awoke. Looking on the Prince with tender eyes, she said, "Is it you, my Prince? I have waited a long time."

The Prince, charmed with these words, and even more with the manner in which they were spoken, knew not how to show his joy and thanks. He vowed he loved her better than he did himself.

The Prince and Princess talked for four hours together, and yet they said not half of what they had to say.

Meanwhile all the palace awoke. Everyone thought about his own business. And, as they were not all in love, they were dying of hunger. The chief maid of honor grew very impatient and told the Princess loudly that supper was served.

The Prince then helped the Princess to rise. She was dressed magnificently, and His Royal Highness took care not to tell her she was dressed like his great-grandmother. She looked not a bit the less beautiful for all that.

Into the great hall of mirrors they went to

dine. Violins and oboes played old tunes. The music was excellent, though it was now above a hundred years since the instruments had been played.

After supper, without losing any time, the Prince and Princess were married in the chapel of the palace.

In two years, the Prince's father died. The Prince and Princess became the new King and Queen, and were given a royal welcome at the capital.

Drakestail

DRAKESTAIL was very little. That is why he was called Drakestail. But this tiny duck had brains, and he knew what he was about. He had started out in the world with nothing, yet he had managed to collect a fortune of a hundred pieces of silver.

Now the King, who was a spendthrift and never kept any money, heard that Drakestail had this fortune. One day he called on the little duck to see about borrowing it. And Drakestail was quite proud of being able to lend money to the King.

But after one year and then another, seeing that the King never dreamed of paying back the loan, Drakestail became uneasy. At last, he decided to go see His Majesty himself, and get repaid.

So one fine morning Drakestail, very smart-looking and gay, took to the road singing, "Quack, quack, quack, when shall I get my money back?"

He had not gone far when he met his friend Fox, on his rounds that way.

"Good morning, neighbor," said this friend. "Where are you off to, so early?"

"I am going to the King to try to get what he owes me."

"Oh, take me with you."

Drakestail said to himself, One can't have too many friends.

"I will," said he to Friend Fox, "but if you walk on all fours you will soon be tired. Make yourself quite small; get into my throat—go into my gizzard—and I will carry you."

"Happy thought!" said Friend Fox.

He took up his bags and baggage and, *presto!* He went down like a letter into a mail slot.

Drakestail was off again, all smart-looking and gay, still singing, "Quack, quack, quack, when shall I get my money back?"

He had not gone a hundred steps when he met his friend Ladder, leaning on her wall.

"Good morning, my duckling," said Friend Ladder. "Where away, so bold?"

"I am going to the King to get what he owes me."

"Oh, take me with you!"

Drakestail said to himself, One can't have too many friends.

"I will," said he to Friend Ladder, "but with your wooden legs you will soon be tired. Make yourself quite small; get into my throat—go into my gizzard—and I will carry you."

"Happy thought!" said Friend Ladder, and nimbly, bag and baggage, she went to keep company with Friend Fox.

"Quack, quack, quack..." Drakestail was off

again singing, and as smart-looking as before. A little farther on he met his friend River, wandering quietly in the sunshine.

"My cherub," said she, "where away so alone, with your tail up like a trumpet, on this muddy road?"

"I am going to the King, you know, for what he owes me."

"Oh, take me with you!"

Drakestail said to himself, One can't have too many friends.

"I will," said he to Friend River, "but you who sleep while you wander will soon be tired. Make yourself quite small; get into my throat—go into my gizzard—and I will carry you."

"Happy thought!" said Friend River.

She took up her bags and baggage, and *glug, glug, glug,* found a place between Friend Fox and Friend Ladder.

"Quack, quack, quack..." Drakestail was off again, singing.

A little farther on he met Comrade Wasp's
Nest, managing his wasps.

"Well, good morning, friend Drakestail," said
Comrade Wasp's Nest. "Where are you bound
for, so smart-looking and gay?"

"I am going to the King to get what he owes
me."

"Oh, take me with you!"

Drakestail said to himself, One can't have too
many friends.

"I will," said he to Comrade Wasp's Nest, "but
with your army to drag along, you will soon be
tired. Make yourself quite small; go down my
throat, into my gizzard—and I will carry you."

"Happy thought! A good idea!" said Comrade
Wasp's Nest.

And, left file, march! He took the same road
to join the others, with all his party. There was
not much more room, but by sitting closer they
managed.

"Quack, quack, quack..." Drakestail was off
again, singing.

Drakestail arrived thus at the King's city, and made his way right up the main street, still running and singing, "Quack, quack, quack, when shall I get my money back?" till he came to the palace.

He rapped with the knocker, *toc! toc!*

"Who is there?" asked the doorman, putting his head out of his window.

"It is I, Drakestail. I wish to speak to the King."

"Speak to the King! That is easily said. The King is dining, and he does not like to be disturbed."

"Tell him that it is I, and I have come he well knows why."

The man shut his window and went up to tell this to the King, who was just sitting down to dinner, with his napkin at his neck. All his ministers were with him.

"Good, good!" said the King, laughing. "I know what it is! Have him come in, and put him with the turkeys and chickens."

The doorman went down again.

"Be good enough to come," he said to Drakestail.

Good, thought Drakestail to himself—now I shall see how they eat at court.

"This way, this way," said the doorman. "One step farther. There, there you are!"

"How? What? In the poultry yard?"

How angry Drakestail was! "Ah, so that's it," said he. "Wait! I will *make* you receive me! Quack, quack, quack, when shall I get my money back?"

But turkeys and chickens are creatures that don't like people who look different from themselves. When they saw how this newcomer looked, and when they heard him singing, too, they began to give him black looks.

"What is it? What does he want?" they cried.

Finally they all rushed at him, to peck him to death.

I am lost! said Drakestail to himself. Then by good luck he remembered his comrade, Friend Fox, and he cried:

"Reynard, Reynard, hurry, friend,
Or Drakestail's life is at an end."

Then Friend Fox, who was only waiting for these words, hastened out. He threw himself on the wicked fowls, and *quick! quack!* he tore them to pieces. In five minutes not one was left alive.

Drakestail, quite happy again, began to sing, "Quack, quack, quack, when shall I get my money back?"

When the King, who was still at table, heard this, and when the poultry woman came to tell him what had been going on in the yard, he was terribly angry. He ordered them to throw this tail of a drake into the well, to make an end of him.

This was done, just as he ordered.

Drakestail was despairing of getting out of so deep a hole when he remembered his friend Ladder, and called:

"Ladder, Ladder, hurry, friend,
Or Drakestail's life is at an end."

Friend Ladder, who was only waiting for these words, hastened out. She leaned her two arms on the edge of the well. Drakestail climbed nimbly on her back, and hop! He was in the yard, where he began to sing more loudly than ever.

When the King, who was still at table and laughing at his trick, heard Drakestail again calling for his money, he was full of rage. He commanded that the furnace should be heated and this tail of a drake thrown into it, because he must be a wizard.

The furnace was soon hot, but this time Drakestail was not so afraid. He counted on his friend River.

"River, River, come out, friend,
Or Drakestail's life is at an end."

Friend River hastened out, and *rrrouf!* She threw herself into the furnace, which she flooded —and, with it, all the people who had lighted it. After this, she flowed growling into the hall of the palace, with her water up to a height of more than four feet.

Drakestail, quite content, began to swim, and to sing deafeningly, "Quack, quack, quack, when shall I get my money back?"

The King was still at table, and thought himself quite sure of his game. But when he heard Drakestail singing again and heard all that had happened, he became furious. He got up from the table, shaking his fists.

"Bring him here and I'll cut his throat! Bring him here at once!"

Quickly two footmen ran to fetch Drakestail.

"At last," said the poor chap, going up the great stairs, "they have decided to receive me."

Imagine his terror when he saw the King, as red as a turkey cock, and all his ministers standing up with swords in hand. This time he thought it was all up with him. Happily, however, he remembered that there was still one remaining friend, and he cried in a dying kind of voice:

"Wasp's Nest, Wasp's Nest, hither, friend,
   Or Drakestail's life is at an end."

Now everything changed.

"Bzz, bzz, bayonet them!" The brave Wasp's
Nest rushed out with his army of wasps. They
threw themselves on the angry King and his ministers and stung them so fiercely that they lost
their heads. Not knowing where to hide, they all
jumped pell-mell from the window and broke
their necks on the pavement.

Now behold Drakestail—most astonished, and
all alone in the big hall as master. But he remembered why he had come to the palace. He set to
work hunting for his money. In vain he rum-
maged in all the drawers. He found nothing. All
had been spent.

Searching this way from room to room, Drakestail came at last to the room with the King's
throne in it. Feeling weary, he sat down on it to
think over his adventure.

By now the people had found their King and
his ministers on the pavement, with their feet in

the air. They went into the palace to find out
how this had happened.

In the throneroom the crowd saw someone on
the royal seat. They broke out, in cries of surprise and joy:

"*The King is dead, long live the King!*
Heaven has sent us this new King!"

Drakestail, who was no longer surprised at anything, received these words of the people as if he
had been hearing such words all his life.

A few people murmured that a Drakestail
would make a fine King! Those who knew him
said that a wise Drakestail was a more worthy
King than a spendthrift person like the one lying
on the pavement.

So the people ran and took the crown off the
head of the dead King and placed it on Drakestail,
whom it fitted perfectly.

Thus Drakestail became King.

"And now," he said after this ceremony,
"ladies and gentlemen, let's go to supper. I am
so hungry!"